About the Author

Munro Leaf created hundreds of Watchbird cartoons over a twenty-two year period in the 40s and 50s. These are the best of the flock that made Mr. Leaf's name a household word at that time. Today Munro Leaf is probably best known for *The Story of Ferdinand*, but he wrote over forty books and illustrated many more, too. For more information on Munro Leaf, see the *Afterword* of this book.

Four-and-Twenty Watchbirds

Four-and-Twenty Watchbirds

by
Munro Leaf

Linnet Books
Hamden, Connecticut

©1939, 1941, 1944, 1946 Munro Leaf
©1990 Estate of Margaret Leaf. All rights reserved.

Published 1990 as a Linnet Book,
an imprint of The Shoe String Press, Inc.
Hamden, Connecticut 06514

Library of Congress Cataloging-in-Publication Data

Leaf, Munro, 1905–
    Four-and-twenty watchbirds / by Munro Leaf.
        p.   cm.
    Summary: Humorous illustrations of the Watchbirds help to introduce the rules of etiquette.
    ISBN 0-208-02208-2
    1. Children—Conduct of life.   2. Etiquette for children and teenagers.   [1. Etiquette.   2. Conduct of life.]   I. Title.
II. Title: 4 and 20 watchbirds.
BJ1631.L4515   1990
395'.122—dc20   89-49742

The text and illustrations of Watchbirds in this book originally appeared in four volumes by Munro Leaf, from which these are a selection: *The Watchbirds: A Picture Book of Behaviour; Fly Away, Watchbird!; Flock of Watchbirds;* and *Three-and-Thirty Watchbirds.*

Printed in the U.S.A.
Designed by Marie-Louise Scull

Foreword

When parents and grandparents look back honestly at their own childhood days, they admit that like all children always and everywhere, they were not perfect. They had to learn *not* to do some things — like pulling the cat's tail, or pouting, or being sneaky, or telling lies. And when they lost these bad habits, they grew up a little bit more.

But what children today don't know is that

THEY HAD HELP.

They had a flock of little Watchbirds looking out for them, and each Watchbird carefully watched all their bad behavior, until it was watched away.

In fact, these Watchbirds were so successful in helping your parents and grandparents grow up, we have asked twenty-four of them back to fly into this book for you.

When you look in these pages you will probably recognize some of the creatures the Watchbirds watch. Maybe you know one, or even two. Not many children would want to live with them, and not many children would want to *be* one. They don't have much fun, as you can see. But when the Watchbirds arrive, these characters usually disappear, and some more grown-up children take their places. And when that happens, the Watchbirds fly away.

Can you guess why?

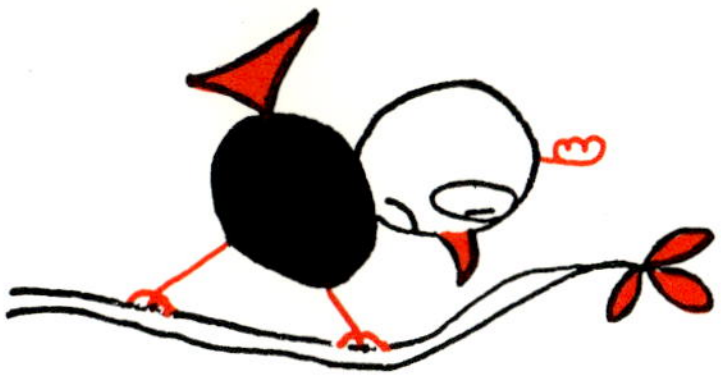

THIS IS A WATCHBIRD WATCHING A SQUAWKER

THIS IS A SQUAWKER

This is a Squawker having a fit of temper. It looks as though it were trying to swim on the floor, because every time it doesn't get its own way it squawks and kicks its feet so fast that nobody can tell how many legs it has. It just doesn't make any sense at all.

WERE YOU A SQUAWKER TODAY?

THIS IS A WATCHBIRD
WATCHING A
WON'T-WASH

THIS IS A WON'T-WASH

This Won't-wash never washed its face or hands or brushed its teeth or combed its hair. Now at last it is ready to use a toothbrush and comb, but it is almost too late. It has only one tooth left and the birds have made a nest in its hair.

WERE YOU A WON'T-WASH TODAY?

THIS IS A BUTTER-IN

THIS IS A WATCHBIRD WATCHING A BUTTER-IN

It butts in every time somebody is talking and never waits for them to finish what they have to say. This one has butted in so many times that it has sprouted horns and a beard just like a goat.

WERE YOU A BUTTER-IN TODAY?

THIS IS A WATCHBIRD WATCHING A
FOOD FUSSER

THIS IS A FOOD FUSSER

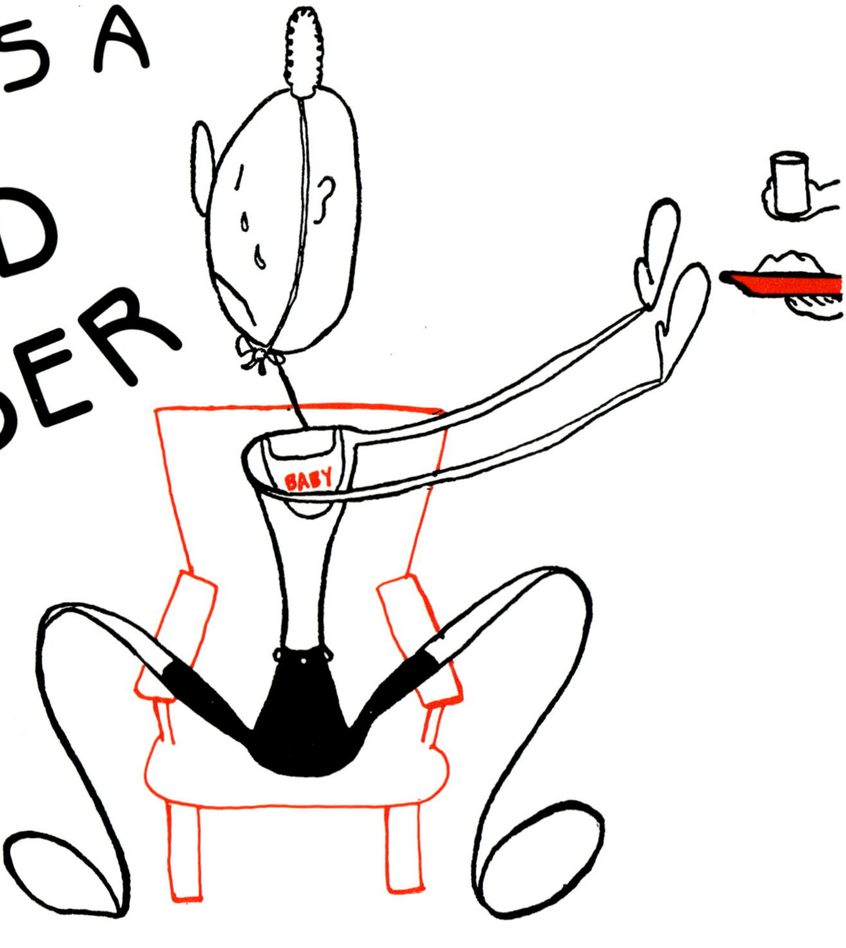

who is much too old to be still sitting in a baby chair, but it fussed about what is should eat so much that it doesn't eat anything now and it is so thin that it isn't strong enough to get up.

WERE YOU A FOOD FUSSER TODAY?

THIS IS A WATCHBIRD
WATCHING A
WON'T-SHARE

THIS IS A WON'T-SHARE

This person that looks like a pig is a Won't-share. It never gave anything that it owned to anybody. It keeps its toys and books and games and everything to itself and never lends or shares them. Right now it is so afraid somebody might ask it for one of those two lollipops, it can't enjoy either of them. What a sad pig!

WERE YOU A WON'T-SHARE TODAY?

THIS IS A PLOTTER

THIS IS A WATCHBIRD WATCHING A PLOTTER

This objectionable creature who is trying to look so wise, but isn't, is a Plotter. It is never happier than when it is spoiling other people's friendships. If it finds two people who like each other it whispers and tells tales until they are afraid to trust each other any more. Plotters are mean and shouldn't have any attention paid to them.

WERE YOU A PLOTTER TODAY?

THIS IS A WATCHBIRD WATCHING A BORROWER

THIS IS A BORROWER

This Borrower always uses somebody else's things and never remembers to take them back. It finally had so many things that didn't belong to it, its mother made it promise to return them. But now it has waited so long it has forgotten whose they are — even the bicycle!

WERE YOU A BORROWER TODAY?

THIS IS A WATCHBIRD WATCHING A FLOOR-PILER

THIS IS A FLOOR-PILER

Floor-pilers never pick anything up — their towels, their toys, their clothes, or their books. This one went a whole year without picking anything up, and the room got so full the Floor-piler couldn't even pick itself up.

WERE YOU A FLOOR-PILER TODAY?

THIS IS A WATCHBIRD WATCHING A **BATHROOM-WRECKER**

THIS IS A **BATHROOM-WRECKER**

When Bathroom-wreckers are through with a bathroom nobody else even wants to go in there. They let tubs run over, drop all the towels and washcloths on the floor, leave black rings in toilet bowls, waste the soap, leave the bathroom glass dirty, and make a mess of everything. And just to make things worse, they always squeeze the toothpaste tube from the wrong end and never put the cap back on.

WERE YOU A BATHROOM-WRECKER TODAY?

THIS IS A WON'T-TRY

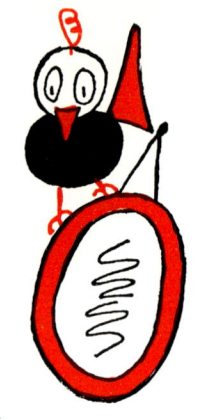

THIS IS A WATCHBIRD WATCHING A

WON'T-TRY

This sad-looking creature plopped down on the stool is a Won't-try. It will never try to do anything new, but just gives up and cries before it even tries to see if it can. This Won't-try was supposed to dress itself, and all it will do is sit there and squawk, "I can't, I can't." What a pity!

WERE YOU A WON'T-TRY TODAY?

THIS IS A NOT-SO

THIS IS A WATCHBIRD WATCHING A NOT-SO

This is a Not-so, who almost never tells the truth. It fibs and lies and tells so many things that are not true at all that nobody knows when to believe it. This Not-so has just said that it doesn't know where its sister's doll or its brother's tennis racket is.

It is very sad to be a Not-so.

WERE YOU A NOT-SO TODAY?

THIS IS A KNOW-IT-ALL

THIS IS A WATCHBIRD WATCHING A KNOW-IT-ALL

This smarty with its nose up in the air is a Know-it-all, and it won't listen to anyone. It thinks it knows all there is to know, and nobody can tell it a thing. This Know-it-all's mother just told it to be careful and it said, "Pooh-pooh!" But it won't say much of anything when it hits the bottom of that hole.

WERE YOU A KNOW-IT-ALL TODAY?

THIS IS A FLIPPERTY

THIS IS A WATCHBIRD WATCHING A FLIPPERTY

Flipperties never help. They sing and dance and play all day, but when there is work to do, they run away from it and somebody else has to do it. People get very tired of Flipperties because they aren't fair.

WERE YOU A FLIPPERTY TODAY?

THIS IS A STUBBORN

THIS IS A WATCHBIRD WATCHING A STUBBORN

Stubborns are the most senseless things you'll ever meet. They just won't do the right thing no matter what, and most of the time they don't even know why they won't. This Stubborn wouldn't do one thing it should all day yesterday even if it wanted to itself, and this morning it is being so stubborn it won't get up and start a new day. It just sits there crying and stupidly saying "No-no-no" to everything.

WERE YOU A STUBBORN TODAY?

THIS IS AN I-WON'T

THIS IS A WATCHBIRD WATCHING AN I-WON'T

No matter what you ask it to do, the only answer you'll ever get out of this stupid thing is, "I won't." It is just plain disobedient and says "No" before it even hears what you want it to do. This I-won't doesn't know what it's missing. Somebody said, "Come here, please," and it shouted, "I won't!" before it heard the rest. All the other person wanted was to ask if it would like to go to the circus. So now the I-won't won't.

WERE YOU AN I-WON'T TODAY?

THIS IS A
WATCHBIRD
WATCHING A
BRAGGER

THIS IS A BRAGGER

To hear Braggers tell about themselves, you'd think they were the most wonderful people in the world. They squawk, yap, and blah about how great they are until everybody gets sick and tired of them. This Bragger just squashed a caterpillar, and the way it is telling about it, you'd think it had killed a dangerous monster.

WERE YOU A BRAGGER TODAY?

THIS IS A WATCHBIRD WATCHING A PESTER

THIS IS A PESTER

This is a Pester, and what a whining, wanting nuisance it is. Pesters are always asking for things they can't have, or wanting to do something they shouldn't. When they are told "No," that doesn't stop them. They keep right on pestering and pestering and begging and begging until they make others wish that they had never seen a Pester.

WERE YOU A PESTER TODAY?

THIS IS A WATCHBIRD WATCHING A TATTLETALE

THIS IS A TATTLE-TALE

It goes around minding everybody's business but its own. It screams and yells, "Look what So-and-So did wrong," but it never tells anyone what it did wrong. Tattletales are just plain annoying.

WERE YOU A TATTLETALE TODAY?

THIS IS A WATCHBIRD WATCHING A GRABBER

THIS IS A GRABBER

Grabbers are not liked by anyone. Every time a Grabber sees something it wants, it just grabs and never asks if it may have it, never says "Please," and never shares with anyone. No wonder Grabbers look weird and no one likes them.

WERE YOU A GRABBER TODAY?

THIS IS A WATCHBIRD WATCHING A **POUTER**

THIS IS A POUTER

This is a Pouter that pouts and whines whenever it doesn't have its own way. If it can't go somewhere that it shouldn't or do something it shouldn't, or have something it shouldn't, that lip begins to stick out and that lump gets in its throat, the tears begin to roll, and how it pouts and whines. It is terrible.

WERE YOU A POUTER TODAY?

THIS IS A WATCHBIRD WATCHING A **BULLY**

THIS IS A BULLY

Nobody likes a Bully because it always picks on people who are smaller and weaker than itself. If it can't find somebody smaller than it is, it will even pick on animals. No wonder nobody likes it!

WERE YOU A BULLY TODAY?

THIS IS A WATCHBIRD
WATCHING A
SHOW-OFF

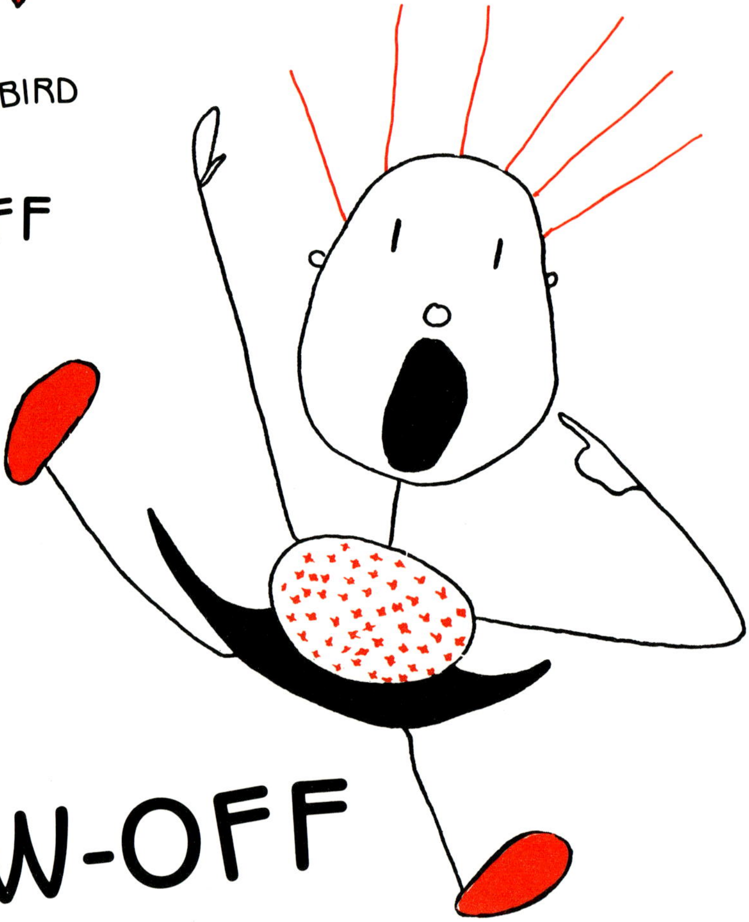

THIS IS A SHOW-OFF

This is a Show-off. It is never happy unless everyone is watching it all the time. It screams, it jumps, it struts and yells, "Look at me!" until everybody thinks it's just plain boring.

WERE YOU A SHOW-OFF TODAY?

THIS IS A WATCHBIRD
WATCHING A
SNEAKY

THIS IS A
SNEAKY

A Sneaky is not the sort of person anybody likes. Sneakies never will admit that they have done anything wrong, but try to pretend it was always somebody else's fault. This Sneaky just broke its mother's best flower vase and it's been hiding behind the chair for a long time. Now it has just seen the cat and is thinking maybe it can blame the poor cat.

WERE YOU A SNEAKY TODAY?

THIS IS A WATCHBIRD WATCHING A TOO-LATE

THIS IS A TOO-LATE

It always means to do things on time, but it puts off and puts off doing *what* it should *when* it should, so that it is always late. This Too-late was supposed to go with the others to the movies, but it dawdled and dawdled until it was too late. They left it.

WERE YOU A TOO-LATE TODAY?

Afterword

About Munro Leaf . . . .

At age ten, Munro Leaf told his mother that he had decided to work for himself when he grew up. Like Ferdinand the Bull, a character he was to create in later life, Munro greatly valued the right to be true to himself. Perhaps that is why his books encourage children to treat each other, adults, and animals with the respect and care that they would like for themselves.

As his son I always looked forward to his bedtime stories and never felt a sense of reproof in his fable-like tales or his Watchbird drawings. To the contrary, he made my brother and me laugh, and inspired us to think up Watchbirds for him. These were published one by one for twenty-two years in the *Ladies Home Journal*, and were collected into four books. All in all my father wrote more than forty books, and he avoided moralizing by telling good, simple stories, and using his childlike drawings to convey his ideas. He did not sentimentalize children or speak down to them, and they responded to his

humor, common sense, and genuine concern. *The Story of Ferdinand*, now fifty years old, is ever popular because of this.

Munro Leaf was a passionate and patriotic American. He served as an army officer throughout World War II; he helped to write some of President Roosevelt's "fireside chats"; he worked later with President Johnson's War on Poverty; and he made three cultural exchange tours for the U.S Department of State. But his devotion to children extended to all nations — his books have been translated into no fewer than sixty-five languages! As a child, I remember the United Nations Assembly asking him to write a book explaining that organization to the children of the world, and I remember my joy that *all* children would get to know my father as I did.

Now, as I read his books to my own son, I realize that Munro Leaf's love of children and his ability to amuse them *and* make them mindful of the needs of others, endures today.

James G. Leaf
Director, The Los Angeles
Childrens' Museum